This
David Bennett Book
belongs to

_____

_____

_____

_____

For Regan, Calum and Morgan
J C

First published in 1993 by
David Bennett Books Ltd,
94 Victoria Street, St Albans,
Herts, AL1 3TG

BRITISH LIBRARY CATALOGUING IN PUBLICATION DATA
A catalogue record for this book is available
from the British Library
ISBN 1 85602 028 2

Typesetting by Type City
Production by Imago
Printed in Hong Kong

The Boy who Ate the Sun

Jon Cramer

David Bennett Books

There was once a little boy who loved the sun.

He loved it so much that he decided to eat it.

So he took the longest ladder he could find,
and began to climb, and climb, and climb.

When he reached the top,
he began to cut the sun into slices.

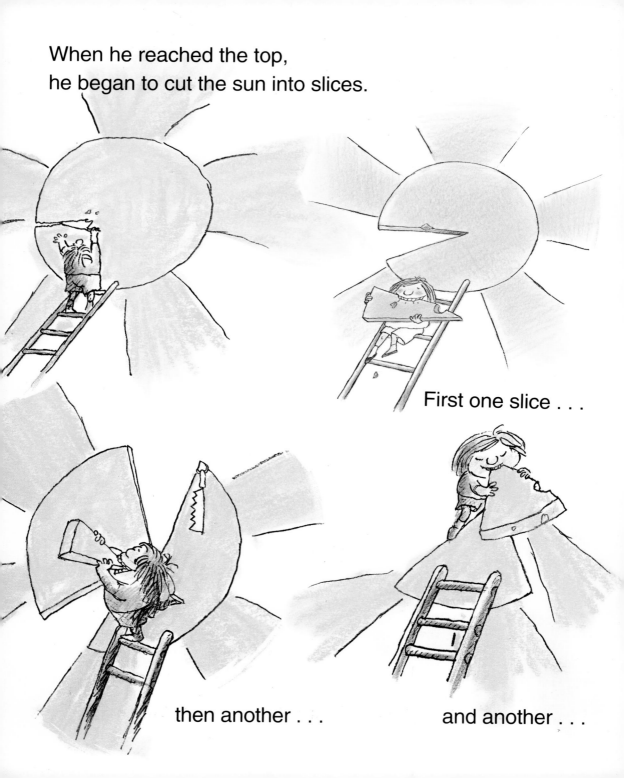

First one slice . . .

then another . . .

and another . . .

until he had eaten it all, right down to the last sunbeam.

It was the fastest sunset the world had ever seen.

When the boy opened his eyes,
huge rays of sunlight shone out
in all directions.

 'Wow!' he thought. 'This is great!'
He rode along looking all around him,
and the great beams of light swept across the countryside.

Terrified rabbits dashed into their burrows.
Frightened birds flew home to their nests.
Finally, he reached a little town.

The people in the town were terrified.
First of all the sun had disappeared and the world had
gone black. Now this strange boy with shining eyes
had arrived out of nowhere.

They locked their doors and hid.

The little boy peered in at people's windows.
  'Peepo!' he shouted, but no one replied.

He knocked on people's doors.
  'Hello!' he shouted, but no one replied.

He climbed the highest chimney in town.
    'Yoo hoo!' he shouted, but no one replied.
Soon the little boy began to tire of his game.
It was no fun playing on his own.

He sat down in the town square, feeling very sorry
for himself.

The mayor, braver than the other townsfolk,
came up to the little boy.
   'What's going on here?' he demanded.
A great golden tear ran down the boy's cheek.
   'I ate the sun,' he sobbed.
   'Ah!' said the Mayor. 'Well, I can't help you,
but I know somebody who can – you must go
to the Wizard of the Dark Woods.'

He helped the little boy on to his horse
and sent him on his way.

The little boy went deeper and deeper into the thick,
dark forest, until he reached a strange castle.

Fearfully, he went up to the front door
and banged the knocker twice.

The door slowly opened, and there in the hallway stood a funny old man.

'You're a bright-looking lad!' he cried. 'Come in!'

'Goodness, I need to find something to shade that bright light.'

'Try this.'

'That won't do.'

'I don't think so.'

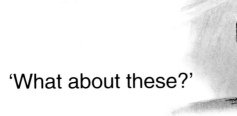

'What about these?'

'Brilliant!'

The Wizard and the little boy sat down together,
and the little boy told the Wizard
exactly what had happened.

'Let me have a good look at you and see what we can do.'

'No problem at all,'
said the Wizard,
and he began to mix
one of his magic potions.

Late that night,
the potion did its work.
The little boy
suddenly woke up.
He tugged on
his clothes, and
dashed outside . . .

across the garden
to a small wooden hut.

Just in time!
But then . . .

The ground began to rumble and roar.
The little boy ran for his life.

'Come on!' yelled the Wizard.

'May I suggest,' said the Wizard,
'that you don't do anything like that ever again?'

But the little boy was far too busy to listen.
  'Look!' he said. 'The moon's come up!
I really love the moon . . .'

Have you collected all these *Sparklers*

The Terrible Troll *Andy Cooke*
ISBN 1 85602 030 4

The last troll alive is terrorising young Alice's town.
Everyone flees for their lives. Who can save them?

The Boy Who Ate The Sun *Jon Cramer*
ISBN 1 85602 028 2

A little boy loves the sun so much that he decides to eat it.
But things don't turn out quite as he expects!

Barnyard Bash *Tessa Richardson-Jones*
ISBN 1 85602 025 8

When the farmer and his family go out for the day,
their animals decide to have some fun!

The Purrfect Carpet *David Passes • Norman Johnson* ISBN 1 85602 029 0

Twopence loves Princess Purrfect dearly, but he is so poor – how can he ever win her hand?

Bed Bugs *Stuart Trotter*
ISBN 1 85602 026 6

When Tommy hears noises *inside* his bed, he decides
to investigate – and makes some curious discoveries!

No Such Thing As Monsters *Guy Parker-Rees*
ISBN 1 85602 027 4

'There's no such thing as monsters,' says Wilf's Mum. But is that true?